Looney Tunes Wacky Adventures

EGGS-TINCT

Cracking Up in Prehistoric Times

by Tracey West

Illustrated by Duendes del Sur

SCHOLASTIC INC.

New York Toronto London Auckland Sydney
Mexico City New Delhi Hong Kong Buenos Aires

This book is a work of hysterical fiction. Any similarities to actual historical persons, places, or events are likely to be wacky. In other words: don't use this book for a history report!

Published by Scholastic Inc.,
90 Old Sherman Turnpike,
Danbury, Connecticut 06816.

0-439-56581-2

Printed in the U.S.A.
First printing, October 2003

CONTENTS

What's Up with This Book?

Ehh, what's up, Doc? I'm Bugs Bunny, star of stage and screen. I work at the Warner Bros. Movie Studios—the WB Studio for short. I'm writin' this because The Big Boss of the WB Studio asked me to explain some wacky stuff that has been happening around here. I told him, "There's no way anyone would believe this. Nope. Count me out." But then The Big Boss offered me a bunch of carrots . . . so read on.

It all started when the ACME Space Replacer showed up at the WB Studio. We've used ACME products for years in our shows. That's because ACME makes gizmos that nobody's ever heard of and thingamajigs that do the impossible. So ACME products are right up our alley, and they don't usually surprise us.

This Space Replacer tops them all, though! That's because the Space Replacer can take us to any place at any time—past, present, or future.

Us, by the way, means me and a few of the characters I work with at the WB Studio. We're known as the Looney Tunes.

There's **Daffy Duck,** an all-right guy for someone who's vain, greedy, and hotheaded.

And there's **Tweety,** a sweet, innocent little bird who lives with a sweet little old lady named **Granny**.

But Tweety is no birdbrain. That's because he has to avoid being eaten by Granny's sneaky cat, **Sylvester**.

Then there's **Porky**—an all-around good guy who usually makes a lot of sense—once he gets the words out. That's just a few of us (you'll meet the rest along the way) who have used the Space Replacer. It sounds like a great idea, but there's a catch . . .

. . . ***Ain't there always?***

The catch is that we can travel in time, but we might not get back! In order to return to the WB Studio, we need to wear a special wristwatch thingy when we time-travel. It's called the Re-replacer, and it gives us the facts about where we landed and what's around us. ***(It's handy since we don't always know our history! Who does?)*** But the Re-replacer also tells us the checkpoint—where we have to be at a certain time—so we can get back home. Oh, and everybody who travels has to be at the checkpoint. If we don't *all* make it there in time, we're history—or maybe future.

So, time travel can be a bumpy ride. Like when Tweety was accidentally zapped back to the days of the dinosaurs, and Daffy and I went after him. How was I able to rescue Tweety as well as keep greedy Daffy from bringing a dinosaur egg back with us? Keep reading to find out.

Bugs Bunny

CHAPTER 1
Where's Tweety?

"L-l-l-l-l-l-l-lunch time!" Porky Pig called out as he swung open the cafeteria doors. "My f-f-f-favorite time of day—next to breakfast and dinner."

As usual, the cafeteria on the WB Studio lot was packed. Members of the Looney Tunes cast were taking a break from filming their latest cartoons.

Bugs Bunny slid his tray along the lunch counter. "I'll have a grilled carrot sandwich, please," said the gray rabbit, "and some carrot cake for dessert."

Granny had brought a picnic lunch for

Tweety Bird and Sylvester. The sweet little old lady handed Tweety a tiny bowl. "Here you go, Tweety," Granny said. "Some nice birdseed salad—hold the onions."

"Thanks, Gwanny!" replied the little yellow canary. Meanwhile, Sylvester, Granny's black and white cat, sat next to Tweety and was drooling over the picnic basket.

"I packed something yummy for you, too, Sylvester dear," Granny said. "Sardine-flavored tofu treats."

Sylvester turned and made a face. "Blech! I'd rather chow down on some tender, tasty Tweety Bird instead," he muttered under his breath. But he smiled sweetly at Granny and took the treats. Someday he'd get that bird!

Over by the microwave oven, Porky heated up a bunch of "Waist Away" diet meals. "I'm w-w-w-watching my weight," the chubby little pig said proudly to Granny.

Granny eyed the stack of diet meals and shook her head. "Of course you are, Dear," she told him.

While the Looney Tunes gang munched on lunch, Hank the prop man, entered the cafeteria. It was Hank's job to take care of the stuff that was used on the film sets. Hank had one of the props with him. It was a box the size of a soda machine. A long rod stuck out from one side, and the front of the box had a round red button and a built-in computer keyboard. Hank wiped sweat from his forehead, left the box, and walked up to the lunch counter.

"What's up, Doc?" Bugs asked him. "How are things in the props department?"

"Busy," replied Hank. "I'm on my way to deliver this thing to Stage 51, but I thought I'd grab some lunch first."

"You should try the grilled carrot sandwich," Bugs said.

Just then Daffy Duck burst through the doors. He was talking on his cell phone to his agent.

"This is outrageous!" Daffy screeched. His black feathers bristled. "The Big Boss may be the head of this studio, but he's got to listen to reason. I will *not* host a special called 'When Guppies Attack!' I'm bigger than that, I tell you. I want to be the star of my own reality TV show.

I want to play a detective on a crime show. I want . . . "

Daffy spied the metal box and pressed the large red button. "I want a refreshing beverage!" But the strange metal box was no soda machine. As soon as Daffy hit the button, a laser beam shot out of the long rod, which was pointed right at Tweety.

Zap! The laser beam hit Tweety, and the little bird vanished, just like that.

"Goodness gracious!" Granny cried, wringing her hands. "What has happened to Tweety?"

"Don't look at me," Daffy said. "All I wanted was a soda pop!"

"So what *is* that thing, anyway?" Bugs asked

Hank the prop man.

Hank shrugged. "Beats me. I just lug things around. I don't ask questions."

Then Bugs spotted a white sheet taped to the side of the machine. He tore it down. "These are some kind of instructions," he said. "This thing is called the ACME Space Replacer. It will transport anybody to any place at any time."

"W-w-w-w-wow!" Porky exclaimed.

Bugs looked over the directions:

1. Use the keyboard to type in the place you want to go.
2. Strap the Re-replacer to the wrist of one of the travelers.
3. Have travelers stand in front of the Beam Activator.
4. Press the big red button.

Bugs finished reading the directions.

"Poor Tweety!" Granny said. "The Beam Activator must have been pointed right at him when Daffy pressed the button."

"Oh no!" Daffy protested. "I will not take the blame for this one! Tweety should have been watching where he was standing!"

While Daffy wailed, Bugs got a better look at the Space Replacer. He noticed a small door near the red button. He opened it up to find a device that looked kind of like a wristwatch. It had a small, square screen instead of a watch face, one black button, and one white button. The word **RE-REPLACER** was stamped onto the wristband.

"Pretty nifty," Bugs said. "I could use a new watch." He strapped the Re-replacer to his wrist and held out his arm, admiring it.

"Well, isn't somebody going to do something about poor Tweety?" Granny said. "Tweety has to be back on the set in three hours."

An idea popped into Daffy's head. He turned

his back on the others while he perfected his plan. "This is my big chance," Daffy said, rubbing his hands together. "The Big Boss will give me a three-picture deal when he finds out I've rescued that little twerp. I'll be a hero!"

Daffy turned back to the group and cleared his throat. "I am obviously the only one here brave enough to rescue Tweety," he said. He grabbed the Re-replacer off Bugs's wrist and stepped in front of the Beam Activator. "Sylvester, press the red button."

"Ha!" Bugs laughed. "Who are you kiddin'? You couldn't save a fish from drownin'."

"Oh yeah?" Daffy shot back. "Do you think *you* can save Tweety? You're nothing but a bucktoothed, bushy-tailed bunny rabbit!"

"Am not!" Bugs yelled.

"Are too!" Daffy yelled back.

"Am not!"

"Are too!"

"Am too!" Bugs cried out, tricking Daffy.

Sylvester rolled his eyes. Bugs and Daffy could be so annoying! With a smirk, he pressed the red button.

The laser beam shot out from the Beam Activator, zapping Bugs and Daffy.

"*Are not!*" Daffy yelled. "And that's final."

Bugs was quiet. Something wasn't right.

"Ha!" Daffy said. "I win!"

"Uh, Daffy," Bugs said slowly. "Something tells me we ain't in Kansas anymore."

"What do you mean? We were never *in* Kansas. We were in the WB—" Daffy stopped and stared.

They were definitely not in the WB Studio cafeteria, either. They were outside, in a small clearing. Tall, leafy trees surrounded them, towering high over their heads.

And a herd of dinosaurs was stomping right toward them!

"*Help!*" Daffy cried.

CHAPTER 2
Tree for Two

Daffy stepped on Bugs's head and scrambled onto a tree branch hanging overhead.

"Watch it, Doc!" Bugs yelled at Daffy. He jumped up onto the branch, joining Daffy just in time. The dinosaurs surrounded the tree and began chomping on some leaves. Daffy gulped and stared into the eyes of a real dinosaur. It was huge—about as long as a school bus. It had sturdy-looking legs; a curved, beaklike snout; and three sharp horns sticking out from the front of its head.

"They look hungry," Daffy said nervously. "You know, I once saw a special about dinosaurs on the Prehistoric Channel. I'm pretty sure it said that dinosaurs loved to eat rabbit."

"Oh no!" Bugs said. "I saw the same special, and I'm pretty sure it said that dinosaurs love to eat duck!"

"You're wrong," Daffy said. "It's rabbit!"

"Duck!"

"Rabbit!"

"Duck!"

"Rabbit!"

Beep!

"Beep?" Bugs asked. The Re-replacer on Daffy's wrist was making noise. "Hey, that watch thingy is trying to tell us somethin'. Gimme that!" Bugs took the Re-replacer off Daffy's wrist and strapped it to his own. He

pushed the black button, and words appeared on the screen:

WHERE: North America
WHEN: Cretaceous period
WHO: 3 travelers, 1 missing
TIME REMAINING: 2 hours, 51 minutes, 3 seconds
RETURN CHECKPOINT: Tar Pits

"The Contagious period!" Daffy sputtered. "We've got to get out of here. I can't get sick. I'm going to be a movie star!"

"That's *Cretaceous,* not *contagious,* ya dummy," Bugs said. "That means we're in prehysterical, I mean, prehistoric times."

Daffy frowned. "If you're such a genius, then you must know what all that other mumbo jumbo means."

"Luckily, I had the instructions on me when we got zapped here," Bugs said. He pulled out the instruction sheet.

"All travelers must reach the checkpoint by the time indicated on the Re-replacer," Bugs read aloud. *"That means all of you have to go where we tell you, when we tell you, or you're*

never coming back!"

"Oh, that's just great!" Daffy wailed. "We'll never get back now."

"Don't get your feathers ruffled," Bugs said. "We've just gotta find Tweety Bird. Then we have to find the Tar Pits so that we can get beamed back to the studio."

"Oh, yeah? And how are we supposed to do that?" Daffy asked. "We're surrounded by rabbit- and duck-eating dinosaurs, remember?"

Bugs pointed the Re-replacer at the dinosaurs. "Maybe we can zap 'em with this thing."

This time, Bugs hit the white button. The Re-replacer didn't zap the dinosaurs as he had hoped. Instead, the words faded, and a picture of a three-horned dinosaur appeared on the screen. Bugs pressed the button again, and more words appeared.

Triceratops

This dinosaur lived in North America during the late Cretaceous period. Adult Triceratops could grow up to 30 feet long, but fortunately for ducks and rabbits, they only ate plants.

I bet that's a relief, isn't it?

"You can say that again, Bub! Whaddya know?" Bugs said. "These big brutes only eat veggies. I wonder if they know where I can get some carrots around here."

CHAPTER 3
Forest Frenzy

"Never mind the carrots," Daffy said. "This means we can get out of this tree! I'll show those lettuce-munching lamebrains who's boss!"

Daffy swung down from the tree and hopped onto the head of the nearest Triceratops. "Shoo! Scram! Skedaddle!" he cried. "There's an all-you-can-eat salad bar in the next prehistoric forest!"

Startled, the Triceratops herd slowly stomped away from the bushes. Daffy hadn't expected them to start moving. He fell backward off the head of the Triceratops and fell onto the Triceratops beside it. He was bounced from one sharp Triceratops horn to the next.

"Yikes!" "Ow!"

"Ouch!" "Quit it!" "Thud!"

The last Triceratops tromped away, and Daffy fell to the ground below. He stood up, rubbing his sore bottom as Bugs jumped down from the tree. "You sure showed them who's boss," Bugs said, grinning. "I think they got the point. Actually, it looks more like *you* got the point instead!"

"Very funny," Daffy said. "You're just jealous because I was brave enough to stand up to those dinosaurs. Well, listen up, Buddy. I'm taking charge of this operation now. The Big Boss will think *I'm* a hero. And I don't want you stealing any of my glory!"

Bugs shrugged. "Fine with me. I just want to get back to my grilled carrot sandwich before it gets stale."

"You can't fool me," Daffy said. "I know you want to hog the hero act for yourself. Now follow me!" Daffy stomped off, heading for the forest full of trees, strange flowers, and ferns.

Bugs rolled his eyes. He didn't really want to do this. Who knew what lurked in that dark tangle of plants? Still, Bugs needed Daffy if he was ever going to get back to his sandwich. So, Bugs slowly followed Daffy in among the tall trees. Some of the flowers were bigger than Bugs's head.

Soon Bugs came upon a giant red flower that was as big as he was. Two orange things were sticking out of the flower's closed bud—two things that looked an awful lot like duck feet.

"Get me out of here!" The muffled cry came from inside the flower bud. It was Daffy!

Bugs chuckled. "Whaddya know. Looks like our hero needs a hero." He stepped up to the flower bud and knocked on the petals. "Yoo-hoo! Anybody home?"

The flower petals opened, and Daffy slid to the ground, covered with slimy, red goo. "It's a good thing I walked ahead," Daffy said, shaking the goo from his feathers. "I fought that flower before it could attack you."

"You're welcome," Bugs said. "Any sign of Tweety Bird?"

"I'm hot on his trail!" Daffy boasted. "Stick close by. I don't want to lose you again!"

Bugs hated to do what Daffy wanted, but he knew he'd better stick close before Daffy got into any more trouble. Big green leaves brushed against their faces as they walked. Strange sounds echoed around them, but so far, there was no sign of Tweety.

Finally, they came to a riverbank. "Maybe Tweety went for a little swim," Bugs said.

"If anyone finds Tweety, it's going to be me!" Daffy reminded him. He marched up and down the riverbank. "There's got to be a clue somewhere."

Then Daffy stomped up to Bugs. "There's no sign of Tweety here," Daffy said. "Let's get moving."

A strange feeling crept over Bugs. "Did you ever get the feeling that you're bein' watched?" he asked.

"Sure, all the time," Daffy said. "I have adoring fans everywhere!"

But Bugs couldn't shake that feeling. He looked over his shoulder . . . and right into the face of a dinosaur!

"Er, Daffy," Bugs said, tapping him on the shoulder. "Is *that* one of your fans?"

Before Daffy could look, the dinosaur scooped him up in its arms. Then it turned and ran away. ***"Heeeeeeeelp!"*** Daffy wailed.

"Good riddance," Bugs said. "It will be easier to find Tweety by myself."

Bugs took a few steps and then stopped. The operating instructions for the Space Replacer echoed in his mind. *All travelers must reach the checkpoint by the time indicated on the Re-replacer.*

"Oh, brother," Bugs muttered. He pressed the black button on the Re-replacer. Words popped up on the screen:

WHERE: North America
WHEN: Cretaceous period
WHO: 3 travelers, 2 missing
TIME REMAINING: 1 hour, 54 minutes, 25 seconds
RETURN CHECKPOINT: Tar Pits

Bugs sighed. "Guess I'd better go save that duck again," he said. "And find Tweety, too."

CHAPTER 4

Daffy Duckling

Bugs followed the trail that ran alongside the river. He walked up a small hill and looked down. Below, he could see several dinosaurs sitting in a circle. Daffy sat in the center of the circle, looking totally helpless, as usual. One of the dinosaurs picked up Daffy and squeezed him tightly. Another dinosaur grabbed him and began licking Daffy's feathers.

"Stop it, you big beast!" Daffy shouted. "You don't know who you're dealing with! I'm a big star!"

Bugs chuckled and got closer to the nest. "Let's find out more about these dinosaurs,"

Bugs said. He pointed the Re-replacer at a dinosaur, hit the white button, and read these words:

Parasaurolophus

This duck-billed dinosaur had a long, flat tail and strong arms that were probably used for swimming.

A dinosaur with a duck bill? That's pretty daffy-looking, if you ask me.

"Duck-billed, eh?" Bugs chuckled. "I thought those big guys looked familiar.

A Parasaurolophus had grabbed Daffy and was patting him on the head. Daffy's neck bobbed up and down with each pat. "Watch the 'do!" Daffy complained. "I spent three hours having my feathers done this morning!"

"Daffy," Bugs called. "I know you like your fans and all, but we *are* on a schedule here." Bugs turned and began to walk away.

"Wait!" Daffy screamed. "I mean—I told you to stick by me, didn't I? I'm in the middle of questioning these dinosaurs to see if they know where Tweety is. Maybe you could help out a little bit."

Bugs folded his arms and sighed. Why

couldn't Daffy just admit that he needed help? "Okay," Bugs said. "What do you want me to do?"

One of the dinosaurs picked up Daffy and licked him right in the face. The other dinosaurs all made weird cooing noises. "Get these slimy dinosaurs off me!" Daffy yelled. "I can't stand it anymore!" The dinosaur squeezed Daffy tightly in its strong arms.

"Aw, ain't that cute," Bugs said. "They think you're a baby duck-billed dinosaur."

"I am *not* a baby!" Daffy wailed. One of the dinosaurs leaned over and patted Daffy's head again.

Daffy screamed as his head bobbed up and

down. "Do something right NOW!"

"Calm down," Bugs said. "Pretend you're talking to your agent about a movie deal."

"That's ridiculous!" Daffy replied.

Bugs shrugged. "Fine. If you don't think you deserve a movie deal . . . "

"Of course I deserve a movie deal! I'm a huge star!" Daffy began to whine and moan. "It's not fair!" Daffy pouted and stomped his feet on the ground. The dinosaurs looked at each other and made loud, chirping noises. Then they stood up and stomped off toward the river.

Bugs smiled. His plan had worked. Daffy's whining and crying had made the dinosaurs think their baby was hungry, and they had gone off to find him food.

Of course, Daffy didn't see it that way. "Look! I scared them off," Daffy said proudly. "It's a good thing I'm the leader here."

"Whatever you say," Bugs said. "Listen, this whole duck-billed deal has given me an idea about where Tweety might be."

"I don't need *your* ideas!" Daffy snapped. "I've got *plenty* of ideas!"

"Okay," Bugs said. "Let's hear 'em."

Daffy scratched his head and looked thoughtful.

Minutes went by. Bugs tapped his foot while he waited. Finally, Daffy spoke. "Let me hear your idea," he said. "I'll tell you if it's any good."

"Well," Bugs said, "if those dinosaurs thought you were a baby duck-billed dinosaur, then maybe some flying dinosaurs thought Tweety was their baby."

"That's the stupidest idea ever," Daffy said. "Whoever heard of a flying dinosaur, anyway?"

Screech!

Suddenly a dinosaur with a long, thin bill swooped down from the sky. Its leathery wings brushed against Bugs and Daffy. Then the dinosaur took off. Bugs and Daffy watched as

the flying dinosaur circled above a tall cliff. Its nest was on top of the cliff.

"On second thought, that's a brilliant idea," Daffy said, changing his mind. "Glad I thought of it!" he added, as he ran toward the cliff. "Hang on, Tweety! I'm coming to save you!" Daffy cried.

"Here we go again," Bugs said, as he ran after Daffy.

CHAPTER 5
More Egg-citement

Daffy began to climb up the side of the cliff, while Bugs held back. He pointed the Re-replacer at the dinosaur flying overhead and pressed the white button:

Pteranodon

Of all the flying dinosaurs, this was the biggest. It had a wingspan of 23 feet—about as wide as a house. This was the jumbo jet of the dinosaur world.

Bugs shook his head. "Looks like Daffy's headed for some *big* trouble," he said, chuckling. "I'd better make sure that dumb duck doesn't end up as bird food."

The Pteranodon circled the cliff once more and then took off over the forest. "The coast is clear—for now," Bugs said. Then he began to climb up the cliff.

But Daffy was far ahead of Bugs. The duck huffed and puffed as he struggled up the steep cliff. Daffy's feet kicked up dust and rocks that slid down the cliff and bounced off Bugs's head.

"Watch it, Doc!" Bugs called up to Daffy. Then Bugs shook his head. "This is for the

birds," he muttered, looking up the high cliff. Daffy was on his own.

Bugs leaned against a low, flat rock and closed his eyes. Images of food popped into his head. After all, he hadn't eaten lunch. Carrot sandwiches . . . carrot salad . . . carrot cake . . . carrot soup . . . carrot cutlets . . . cream of carrots . . . carrot . . . *plunk!*

"Plunk?" Bugs woke from his daydream as a rock bounced next to him. He looked up to see Daffy running back down the cliff carrying a humongous egg.

"I found it! I found it!" Daffy cried.

"Uh, I hate to break it to you, Daffy, but that ain't Tweety," Bugs said. "Tweety is little and yellow and . . . "

"Of course it's not Tweety. It's my ticket to fortune!" Daffy snapped.

"That ain't a ticket, either," Bugs said. "That's an egg!"

"Not just any egg," Daffy said. "It's a *dinosaur* egg! Don't you see what this means? I can bring this back to our world and hatch it, and then I'll be the proud owner of a *real* dinosaur. I'll make millions charging everyone to see it. I'll be rich! Rich, I tell you!"

"I don't know, Daffy," Bugs said. "That idea seems a little scrambled to me."

"I don't care what *you* think," Daffy shot back. "I'm going to bring this back to our time, and you're not going to stop me!"

"Maybe I won't stop you, Doc," Bugs said, pointing to the sky, "but ***she*** will."

"Huh?" Daffy looked up to see the Pteranodon swoop down from the sky, screeching angrily. Its long, pointed beak and black, beady eyes were aimed right at Daffy.

"That's one angry Mommy Dinosaur," Bugs said.

"Oh no!" Daffy cried. "I'm not giving up my ticket to fortune!" Daffy ran down the cliff, still clutching the egg tightly. Bugs raced after him.

Screeeeeeech!

Bugs looked over his shoulder. The mother Pteranodon was gaining on them. "Daffy, drop the egg!" he yelled.

"Never!" Daffy shouted back.

Screeeeeech!

Bugs could feel the wind on his back from the beating of the Pteranodon's huge wings. "Drop it!" Bugs ordered.

"No!" Daffy stubbornly replied.

Screeeeeech!

The Pteranodon's wings beat loudly in Bugs's ears. It was only a matter of time now.

"Good-bye, cruel world!" he wailed.

Suddenly he saw a welcome sight—a cave at the bottom of the cliff. They were just a few

feet away from it. "Bye, bye, birdie!" Bugs cried.

He dove into the cave, pushing Daffy in ahead of him. They rolled into the cave, tumbling head over heels. Finally, they stopped. Daffy didn't let go of the egg once.

CHAPTER 6
The Dark, Dark Cave

Bugs slowly sat up. Outside, he could hear the angry screeching of the Pteranodon. "Lucky for us, that dino's afraid of the dark," he said. "Now, all you have to do is give her back the egg, and we can get out of here."

Bugs could see the whites of Daffy's eyes gleaming in the darkness. "No, siree," Daffy said stubbornly. "That overgrown chicken can't fly around out there forever. I'll just wait until she's gone."

"That ain't no chicken," Bugs said. "And I don't think we can wait that long." Bugs checked the Re-replacer. Luckily, the screen glowed in the dark. He hit the black button for a report. They only had 23 minutes left! Bugs showed Daffy the screen. "All right, leader," he said. "Got any more bright ideas?"

Daffy frowned. "I am *not* giving up this egg.

There's got to be another way out of this cave. Let's look around."

"In case you haven't noticed, it's dark in here," Bugs pointed out.

"I'm not afraid of a little dark," Daffy bragged. "I'll find Tweety and get us out of here. You'll see."

Bugs sighed and sat back. Eventually, his eyes grew used to the darkness. He watched Daffy creep around the cave like a detective while keeping a tight grip on the egg.

Then Daffy stopped. "Hey, I think I found something," he called out. "It's a tree!"

"I'm no cave expert, but I don't think trees grow in caves," Bugs said.

"Well, how do you explain this?" Daffy snapped. He ran his hand along the rough surface in front of him.

Bugs got closer. He gently tapped something that did look like a thick tree trunk. Then he looked more closely. The tree trunk looked a lot like a leg. A very, very big leg. "Uh, Daffy," Bugs said. "Look up."

Daffy's eyes slowly moved up the trunk of the tree. Then he gasped. Standing next to Bugs and Daffy was a very, very tall dinosaur. It had a long tail, sturdy legs, and two very short arms. Razor-sharp white teeth lined its massive jaws.

The dinosaur had its back to Bugs and Daffy. Drool dripped from its mouth. Bugs saw that the huge beast was bending over something—something small and yellow.

"Help!" Tweety Bird cried.

CHAPTER 7
T-Rex Trouble

Tweety Bird was cornered. The dinosaur drooled over the little bird and, luckily, it hadn't heard Bugs or Daffy speak. Bugs stepped behind Daffy and shoved him toward the giant beast. "You want to be a hero, right?" he said. "Well, here's your chance."

Daffy scrambled back behind Bugs. "Not so fast," he said. "Why don't you check that watch thingy first. Maybe this one's another salad-eater."

Bugs aimed the Re-replacer at the dinosaur and pressed the white button. Words popped up on the screen:

Tyrannosaurus Rex

This fierce dinosaur was one of the biggest meat-eaters to walk the Earth. Despite its large size, scientists believe the T-Rex may have had a very small brain.

Even though it's big and stupid, it's suggested that you scram when this dinosaur comes around.

Bugs chuckled. "Whaddya know, Daffy? It looks like you and this brute have something in common—a small brain."

"That's not funny!" Daffy wailed. "My brain is not small. I've got a big brain. A huge brain!"

"You're a huge nincompoop!" Bugs said. "Thanks to you, we're trapped between two dinosaurs!"

"This is your fault! You're the one who pushed me into this cave in the first place," Daffy yelled.

"That's because you wouldn't let go of that egg!" Bugs yelled back. "It's your fault!"

"Is not!" Daffy shouted.

"Is too!" Bugs insisted.

"Is not!"

"Is not!" Bugs cried, tricking Daffy.

"Is too!" Daffy said. "It's all my fault!"

RAAAAAAAAAAAAAAAR!

Bugs and Daffy jumped. The T-Rex had heard their arguing and turned away from Tweety Bird. Now the huge beast lurched toward them.

Splat! A giant drop of drool splashed on Daffy's head. "Hey, watch where you're spittin', Buddy!" Daffy said crossly.

RAAAAAAAAAAAAAAAR!

The T-Rex stomped across the cave toward Bugs and Daffy. The floor shook.

Bugs and Daffy ran backward toward the cave entrance. "What's your plan now, Hero?" Bugs asked as they ran.

"Uh, I'm thinking of the same plan you're thinking," Daffy said. "So, why don't you tell me what it is?"

Bugs snatched the egg out of Daffy's arms. "This big boy looks hungry," Bugs said. "Let's see if he's in the mood for some scrambled egg."

"No, no, no!" Daffy wailed, chasing Bugs. "It's my ticket to fortune. I won't give it up.

I won't! I won't!"

Bugs was getting closer to the cave entrance. "You'll thank me later," he said, panting.

"I won't give it up!" Daffy cried. "It's mine! All mine!"

Daffy tackled Bugs. The two of them rolled on the ground. Bugs held on tight as Daffy tried to get the egg away from him. The T-Rex stomped closer and closer.

"It's mine!" Daffy shouted.

STOMP!

"Give it up!" Bugs yelled.

STOMP!

"Never!"

STOMP!

Bugs and Daffy lost their grip on the egg. It rolled out the cave entrance and into the sunlight.

Screeeeeeeeech! The mother

Pteranodon swooped down from the sky and picked up the egg in her claws. The huge T-Rex was distracted by the Pteranodon.

"My egg!" Daffy wailed.

"Never mind that," Bugs said. "Now's our chance!" He ran to the back of the cave and scooped up Tweety.

"Thank you, Bugs," Tweety said. "That mean ol' dinosaur was scawing me."

"Hey," Daffy said, running up. "I'm supposed to be the hero, remember?"

"Fine," Bugs said. "Then why don't you get us out of here, Hero?"

"I came in that way," Tweety said, pointing toward a narrow tunnel in the cave wall.

Bugs picked up Tweety and together he and Daffy ran into

the tunnel. Darkness was all around them, but finally, they saw a ray of light up ahead. They came out of the tunnel into a wide green plain.

"Whew!" Bugs said. "*That* was close!"

"It's a good thing I saved us," Daffy said. "Now we can go home."

"We're not home yet," Bugs said. "We still have to get to the Tar Pits."

Bugs checked the time on the Re-replacer. ***"We've only got 6 minutes and 32 seconds left!"***

CHAPTER 8

A Sticky Time in the Tar Pits

"I don't see any tar pits!" Daffy screamed. "We'll be stuck here forever!"

"Excuse me, Daffy," Tweety piped up.

"Not now, Tweety," Daffy snapped. "I'm trying to think of a plan."

"Excuse me," Tweety said again.

"Quiet!" Daffy said. "I'm trying to think!"

"But I tawt I taw some tar pits when that mean

ol' dinosaur was chasing me," Tweety said.

That got Daffy's attention. "Well, why didn't you say so in the first place? Where?"

Tweety pointed to the other side of the wide plains. "Waaaay over there."

"Yikes!" Daffy cried. "Start running!"

The three travelers raced across the plain, but the Tar Pits never seemed to get any closer.

Daffy held his wing to his head and fell to the ground. "I give up!" he wailed. "We might as well get used to living here. If I'm lucky, some scientist in the future will find my fossilized bones, and I'll be a museum display."

Bugs tapped him on the shoulder. "You might want to get up now," he said.

"I told you, it's no use!" Daffy said.

Bugs shrugged. "Okay, but I don't know how those dinosaurs are going to feel about it."

Daffy looked behind him. A herd of dinosaurs was running quickly in their direction. The dinosaurs were much smaller than the others they had met. They ran upright on two legs.

Daffy covered his eyes with his feathers. "We're doomed!"

"Maybe not," Bugs said. He aimed the

Re-replacer at the approaching dinosaurs and pressed the white button:

> ***Ornithomimus***
>
> **This medium-sized dinosaur had an ostrich-like body. It was believed to be a fast runner. Possible prehistoric cousin to the roadrunner.**

"Perfect!" Bugs said. "They're our ticket to the Tar Pits." He stepped aside and waved his hand. "Oh, taxi!" Bugs called out.

The dinosaurs screeched to a stop. Bugs and Tweety hopped onto the back of one dinosaur.

"This is crazy," Daffy said. "It's never going to—" The Ornithomimus herd took off again. Bugs grabbed Daffy's wing just in time and pulled him up.

"Oh, goody!" Tweety chirped happily.

Riding an Ornithomimus wasn't easy. Tweety

and Bugs didn't seem to mind, but Daffy turned bright green from all the bouncing. "I'm not going to sit down for a week," Daffy moaned.

"*If* we get back," Bugs reminded him. He checked the Re-replacer: **10 seconds left!**

Bugs looked up. Just ahead, he could see pools of black, sticky goo. "Almost there!" Bugs said.

Bugs kept an eye on the Re-replacer as they got closer to the Tar Pits.

Five . . . Four . . . Three . . . Two . . .

"*Jump!*" Bugs yelled.

Bugs, Daffy, and Tweety jumped off the Ornithomimus. Bugs landed on his feet. Daffy landed on his face. His bill was covered with sticky tar.

One!

ZAP!

A ball of light shot out of the Re-replacer. Bugs, Daffy, and Tweety vanished!

CHAPTER 9

There's No Place Like Home

Back at the cafeteria, a beam of light shot out of the ACME Space Replacer. In the next instant, Bugs, Daffy, and Tweety appeared.

Granny, Sylvester, and Porky Pig were gathered around the machine. "Thank goodness!" Granny cried. She ran up and hugged Tweety. "I'm so happy you're safe."

"H-h-h-hip, h-h-h-h-hip—Yipee!" Porky sputtered.

"Figures," Sylvester muttered. "I can't eat him *or* get rid of him!"

"Bugs Bunny saved me from a mean ol'

dinosaur," Tweety chirped.

"Aw, shucks," Bugs said, after he put the Re-replacer back. "I was just tryin' to get back to my carrot sandwich. Where is my lunch, anyway?"

Daffy's face turned bright red. Bugs wasn't supposed to get all the credit for saving Tweety. When Daffy opened his beak to tell his side of the story, ***"Mmmmf mmmmf mmmmmmmf!"*** was all that came out. The sticky tar had glued Daffy's beak shut!

Meanwhile, Granny beamed at Bugs. "You shouldn't be so modest, Dear. Wait until The Big Boss hears about this. I'm sure he'll give you a three-picture deal."

Before Daffy could explode, Hank the prop man came back into the cafeteria. He took one look at Daffy and handed him a glass. "You

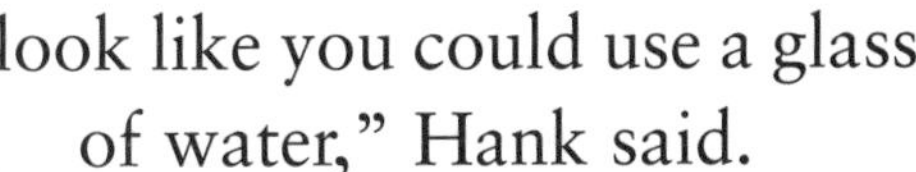

look like you could use a glass of water," Hank said.

Daffy stuck his beak into the glass, and the tar began to wash away.

Granny smiled at Hank. "You can take this nasty machine away now, Dear. Tweety's back safe and sound."

Hank nodded and rolled up his sleeves. "Don't worry, Granny. This'll be locked away on Stage 51 from now on," he said.

"Good riddance!" Bugs said, munching on his carrot sandwich.

"Are you crazy?" Daffy asked when his beak was finally unstuck. "Think of all the riches just waiting for us in other places. We could find gold in Egyptian tombs . . . jewels from pirate chests. It's like our own personal money machine!"

Porky Pig looked thoughtful. "I d-d-d-don't know about treasure," he said, "but I'm sure interested in history. It might be fun to g-g-g-go back in time and see how people lived."

Sylvester didn't say anything out loud, but images of other times and places danced in his mind, too. Times and places

where cats were treated like kings . . . and no one had heard of an annoying little bird named Tweety. He smiled.

Bugs looked at the greedy gleam in Daffy's eye . . . the fascination on Porky's face . . . and Sylvester's sly grin. He shook his head.

"Uh-oh," Bugs said. "Something tells me this ending is only the beginning."